Laura Ingalls Wilder

MY FIRST LITTLE HOUSE BOOKS

WINTER ❧ ON THE ❧ FARM

ADAPTED FROM THE LITTLE HOUSE BOOKS

By *Laura Ingalls Wilder*

Illustrated by *Jody Wheeler and Renée Graef*

■ HARPERCOLLINS PUBLISHERS

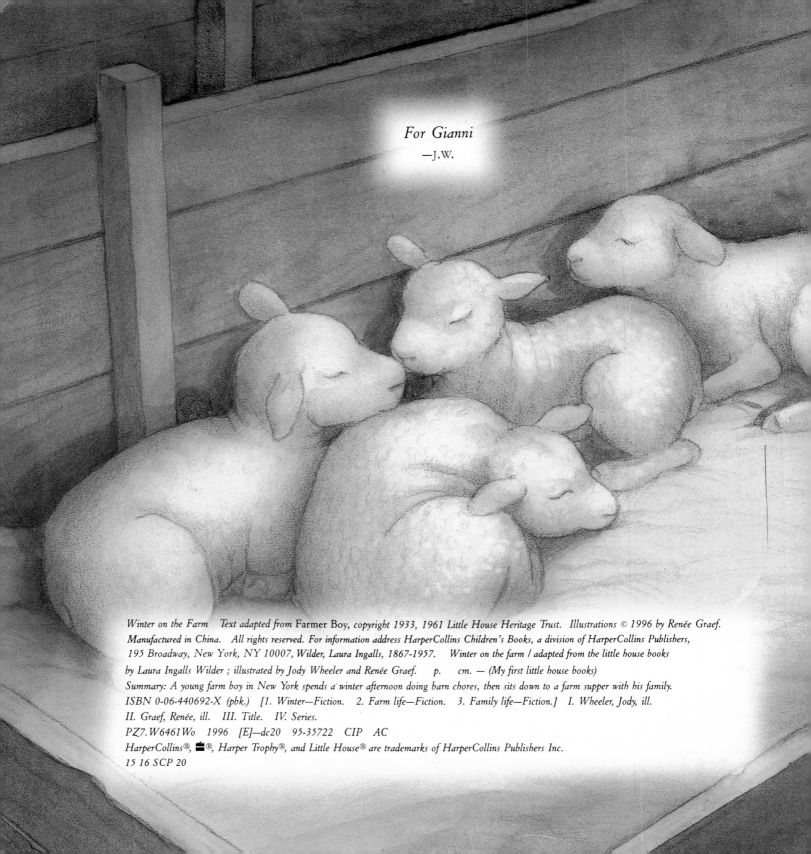

For Gianni
—J.W.

Winter on the Farm   Text adapted from Farmer Boy, copyright 1933, 1961 Little House Heritage Trust.   Illustrations © 1996 by Renée Graef.
Manufactured in China.   All rights reserved. For information address HarperCollins Children's Books, a division of HarperCollins Publishers,
195 Broadway, New York, NY 10007, Wilder, Laura Ingalls, 1867-1957.   Winter on the farm / adapted from the little house books
by Laura Ingalls Wilder ; illustrated by Jody Wheeler and Renée Graef.   p.   cm. — (My first little house books)
Summary: A young farm boy in New York spends a winter afternoon doing barn chores, then sits down to a farm supper with his family.
ISBN 0-06-440692-X (pbk.)   [1. Winter—Fiction.   2. Farm life—Fiction.   3. Family life—Fiction.]   I. Wheeler, Jody, ill.
II. Graef, Renée, ill.   III. Title.   IV. Series.
PZ7.W6461Wo   1996   [E]—dc20   95-35722   CIP   AC
HarperCollins®, ▰®, Harper Trophy®, and Little House® are trademarks of HarperCollins Publishers Inc.
15 16 SCP 20

Illustrations for the My First Little House Books are inspired by the work of Garth Williams with his permission, which we gratefully acknowledge.

Once upon a time, a little boy named Almanzo lived on a big farm in the New York countryside.

Almanzo lived on the farm with his father, his mother, his big brother Royal, and his big sisters Eliza Jane and Alice.

It was wintertime on the farm, and the air was still as ice. The farmhouse roof was covered with snow, and great big icicles hung from the eaves as Almanzo and Royal hurried to the big barn to start their chores.

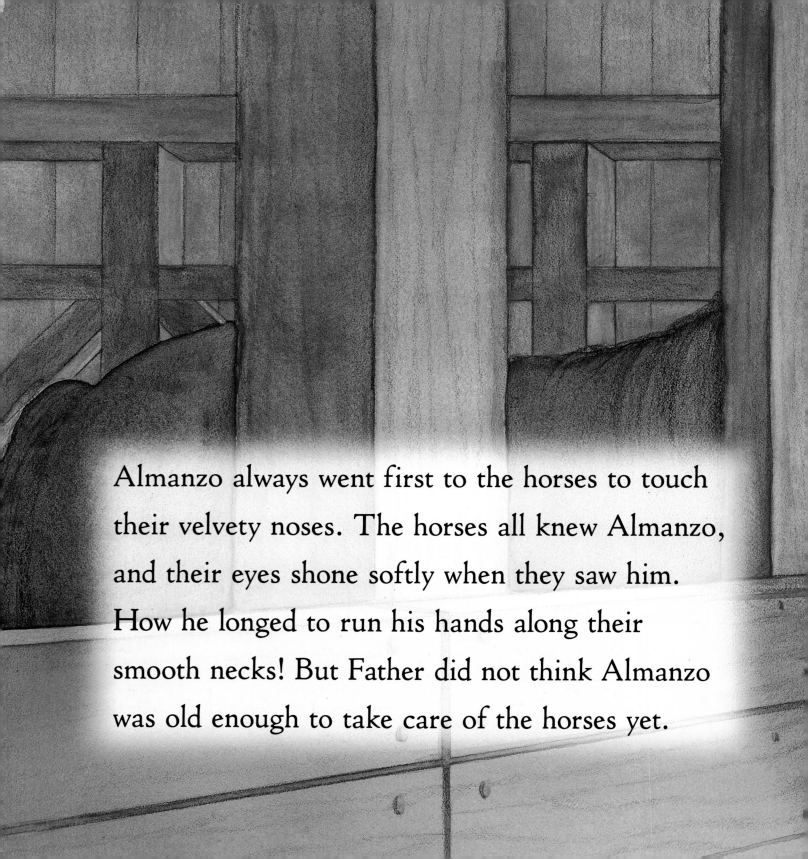

Almanzo always went first to the horses to touch their velvety noses. The horses all knew Almanzo, and their eyes shone softly when they saw him. How he longed to run his hands along their smooth necks! But Father did not think Almanzo was old enough to take care of the horses yet.

So Almanzo put a barn frock on over his good school clothes and went to help Royal make clean beds for the cows and the oxen and the calves and the sheep. They did not have to make beds for the hogs, because hogs make their own beds and keep them clean.

In one stall were Almanzo's own two little calves. One calf had a white spot on his forehead, and his name was Star. The other calf was bright red all over, and Almanzo called him Bright. Almanzo scratched around their little horns, because calves like that.

Next it was time to do the milking. Almanzo took his own milking stool and sat in Blossom's stall to milk her. *Swish, swish!* The milk streamed into the pail, while the cows crunched their carrots and the barn cats purred.

After Almanzo was finished, Father said, "You're a good milker, son." Almanzo kicked at a straw on the floor. He was too happy to say anything.

Almanzo and Royal waited while Father took the
shining tin lantern and made sure that everything
in the barn was snug for the night. Then they
walked through the cold night to the house.
Almanzo was glad to get into the warm kitchen.

First Father, then Royal, then Almanzo took turns washing up at the washbasin. When he was done, Almanzo parted his wet hair and combed it smoothly down.

The kitchen was full of skirts swirling all around.
Eliza Jane and Alice were hurrying to dish up
supper, and Mother was straining the fresh milk.
The salty brown smell of ham frying was making
Almanzo very hungry!

Finally Mother brought the big platter of ham into the dining room, and supper was ready.

Father filled all the plates with food. Almanzo's plate was the very last one to be filled.

Almanzo ate the sweet baked beans and the salt pork. He ate the boiled potatoes and the gravy and the ham. Then he ate the bread and butter and the mashed turnips and the stewed yellow pumpkin. Last of all he ate a large piece of pumpkin pie. Almanzo felt very comfortable inside.

After supper Father brought a big pitcher of cider
and a panful of apples up from the cellar, and Royal
popped some popcorn over the coals in the iron
stove. Mother knitted and rocked, while Eliza Jane
read aloud from the paper and Alice did her sewing.
Almanzo sat by the stove, eating apples and popcorn.

Soon it was time for bed, and Almanzo sleepily climbed the stairs. It was good to be a farmer boy.